Revenge

Marybeth Colton

Contents

Chapter 1

"Honey wake up." my mom whispered shaking my shoulder. I opened my eyes looking into the eyes of my mother who sat on my bed smiling at me "Happy birthday darling" she smiled hugging me tightly "Oh my god I've waited for this day since you were born my baby girl" she smiled kissing my cheek.

today of course was my birthday the day where i'd turn 16 and learn everything..where i'd be moving to in the state, what kind of wolf i'd be alpha, beta, second in comand and lastly i'd find my special someone....my mate the one i'd love forever the one I'd find my heart explode from my chest just by his love.

"I'm happy to mom" I said hugging her back then getting up putting on my glasses then making my way to the bathroom.

Mom smiled and took that as a clue to leave the room making her exit "Happy birthday Liv" she said then made her way out of my room.

I giggled walking into my huge bathroom stripping down to take a quick shower before I got dressed.

When I was done I walked downstairs to see my parents sitting at the dining room table my mom drinking tea while my dad drank his coffee reading the paper. My big brother moved out 2 years ago after he became a werewolf and now lives in Alaska with The Moonlight Path Pack and his mate/wife Stephanie.

I had loved their relationship, how as soon as Jeremy found Stephanie they moved together like they'd never let go....that's exactly what I wanted.

"Happy birthday honey"I heard dad say as I grabbed an apple.

"Thanks dad" I said biting into the apple "Did Jeremy call today?" I asked as I leaned against the counter looking down at the floor.

"No, he didn't sory hun you know he's busy taking care of the pack" mom said sipping her cup of tea as she read her magazine.

I growled and threw my apple acrossed the kitchen where it splattered against the wall "Bull! he's always busy...Too busy for his own sisters sake"! I yelled grabbing my bag and walking out the door "Don't wait up" I said as I walked out feeling my skin burning.

my wolf was screaming inside of my head in fury that our own brother could give a simple call. I growled myself before taking a deep breath and making my way toured the woods in the back yard. Our house was surrounded with woods as I loved it cause my wolf loved to run a lot.

I went to the middle of the woods taking my bag off my shoulder and setting it on the ground, stripping before putting my clothes in my bag and springing into the air turning into my white wolf.

my wolf was a commodity in the Lyca World my mom used to say because of our special fur. Looking at my fur now, I never really thought of my fur as special I just thought of it as Mine.

I grabbed my bag in my mouth carefully as I started to take off in a sprint. I loved running it was the only way to blow off steam without hurting somebody or worse.

I ran as fast as my small paws could carry me, I turned a corner going toured my town wanting to go the way toured my school. I saw two trees next to eachother and smiled my wolfie smile bounding toured them.

Before I could jump something hit me from my side Really hard, throwing me into a tree where I crumpled onto the ground whimpering.

I felt a strong presence and looked up wanting to cower, there was a black wolf in front of me his stance showing power and anger.

Shift! I heard him yell in my head, I cowered but stood slowly. He was twice the size as me making me feel vulnerable. But instead I set my bag down showing I would not waver under his authority.

He looked at me probably wondering why such a small wolf was challenging his authority. He stepped forward which made me step back. He growled stepping forward and grabbing me by the scruff of my neck and biting down a little to har making me whine.

this wouldn't hurt usually but I could tell he was a Alpha of some kind making this stance painful.

I said Shift now or i'll kill you, you're on my territory little wolf! he yelled into my mind letting my scruff go so I could actually breath. I looked up at him and nodded my head. I took my bag behind a tree, at least I had some dignity left. I changed into my human form getting dressed quickly.

I walked back from around the tree seeing a man in front of me, but that didn't surprise me. Most Alphas were male unless they're female and have a lot of Alpha lineage in there family.

I slung my bag over my should, then crossed my arms looking up at him "You're in my Territory little wolf, you better have a good reason" He said his alpha tone high and mighty.

"I...I was on my way to school sir and I wanted to take a shortcut I never realized there was a pack so close to my home before?" I asked looking around the area now being hit by a unfamiliar wolfy smell Wow how couldn't we notice that? my wolf said sounding very dumbfounded.

"Well there is, we just moved here from Alaska you know a change of scenery" he said crossing his muscular arms against his toned chest.

That sentense gave me some hope "Do you know The Moonlight Pack?" I asked excitedly taking a step forward. He looked at me eyeing my "Yes, I am the Alpha" he said looking around the area.

my eyes widened and now I was ticked "Where are you staying?" I asked him anger building up inside.

"In these woods, my pack in large and likes to keep to itself....most of us will be going to the same school as you probably" he said shrugging lightly then yawning "But anyways if you don't mind I don't care if you take this way to school but Never take it again after this or otherwise i'll be forced to report you to your alpha" he said stretching and starting to walk away.

"How can you report me when I don't have an alpha?" I asked looking at his back as it tensed. He turned toured me looking furious "You are a rouge!" he yelled making his way over to me pinning me straight into a tree.

"No...." I choked "I'm un-packed and Un-mated I just turned 16 today" I swallowed hard meeting his eyes, his eyes were charcole black showing his anger.

All werewolves eyes turn black when they're angry it's how we show our anger or pleasure.

"Oh okay that explains it...I'm sorry for pinning you" he said finally letting me go so I could actually breath "Happy birthday by the way, it's a very special day for you little wolf" he said patting my head "What is your name?"

I smiled at his out of the ordinary kindness "Olivia " I said smiling then bowing showing my respect to this alpha.

"Nice to meet you Olivia, I'm Alpha David" he said then bowed back "Have a wonderful day little wolf" he said then turned his head to the side as a howl echowed through the forrest "Excuse me" he said then took off running throwing himself into his wolf form.

I was left in a daze...

Well at least I know I don't have an alpha as a mate.

also I know my brother is in town and he never let me know of his visit.

I was ticked about this fact.

and you should never tick off a she-wolf she'd beat the heck outta you whether you were family or fo

Chapter 2

I finally got to school....Late, walking into my first hour class I walked to my desk with my late slip. I sat in the back wondering who my mate would be? and what he would look like?

I wondered these questions for the rest of the day, going through my classes I looked for him everywhere. Then I found him in the lunch room.

My breath hitched in my throat as Samuel Cliff the next alpha in line to the Misty Moonlight Pack stalked into the lunch room. My eyes roamed over him he wore his usual black long sleeve and jeans that hung dangerously low on his hips. He carried a nice, orderly manner with him as he walked through the lunchroom..

He'd never notice me. I said to myself as I lifted my fork up to take a bite, but that's when my eyes met his. He turned his head toward me not seeming to get the same reaction as me, he just smiled and made his way to his lunch table sitting down and starting the conversation.

I took a deep breath finally taking my eyes off him "I found my mate" I whispered to myself eating a piece of brocoli as I thought. Samuel Cliff was my mate, how was that even possible? I have no beauty what so ever, why would god give him me instead of someone like Jennifer Logan the cheerleading squads captin? or maybe even someone like Lilly Oliver the school slut? at least she'd be prettier than me.

I thought of this as I threw my tray away, I was so out of focus I bumped into my worst enemy, Jamie Collins the Co-cheerleading captin "Move out of the way mutt" she growled as she pushed me to the ground "I don't want to see your filth in my school let alone next to me" she growled then walked away her hips swinging and her heals clicking.

being in a school full of werewolves it was filled of full fledged drama, what non-mated male grabbed a mated males mates butt, who was tougher fighting. This was our drama, but instead of a fist fight, it was full on claws and teeth.

I got up from the ground when Jamie was long gone, not even bothering to grab my tray I made my way out of the lunch room toward the bathroom where I sat staring at myself.

why didn't he feel the connection? my wolf asked me feeling restless in my mind, I couldn't answer her for I didn't know myself, it was something oblivious to me, why my mate wouldn't want to ingulf me in hugs and love me forever...Unless....he rejected me.....

the thought hit me so hard I backed myself up against the wall, it was the only explanation of why he wouldn't go to me after he felt the connection.

He didn't love me, maybe because I wasn't beautiful, maybe because I wasn't the right height or size I wasn't enough to please my mates wants of his mate, That's when tears started flowing down my face, it hurt so bad to think of his possible rejection.

I got up from where I sat and walked out of the bathroom hearing the late bell ring. Great....

I walked into the classroom recieving detention for an hour after school, this wasn't the greatest present I could of received on my birthday.

I walked to my seat then was struck with total realization, Samuel was in the same room with me and was glaring at me from behind, I could feel his eyes burning holes in my back. Looking back I snuck a peek at him, he was staring straight at me with a hand stretched out with a note in it. I reached back grabbing it and setting it on my desk.

my wolf felt fearful but then again I wanted to open it, I unfolded the edges and my heart automatically broke at what I read.

I'd never want you as a mate, I hope you know this. You're nothing an alpha would ever want, you're ugly, pathetic and worthless. I never want to hear the word mate and my name exit your mouth.

Samuel.

I couldn't breath, it felt like my world was crashing down around "Sir could I be excused" I said to our teacher Mr Jackson who stood nodding to me. I got up running out of the room, running toward the exit feeling my heart and lungs collapsing over each other as I ran outside not caring whether I ripped my clothes apart or not.

my wolf took over howling in pain and fury of our mates rejection.

--Samuels   Point   of View---

It hurt like heck when my mate ran out of the room, I didn't want to say that to her but I had to. I had known she was my mate since last year but never had the guts to tell her. But now that I have my fathers will of Alpha on my shoulders, I didn't want to bring her into the dangerous world of being an alphas mate. It would kill my wolf and myself to put her in danger...

I felt as if having her as my mate would put her in danger. My wolf was ticked at me of course, I took his mate away from him and made her feel pain emotionally.

he fought with me inside of my mind, yelling at me How Dare You, you're so selfish, we can protect her! he yelled

I looked out the window seeing her running out toured the woods, that was our wolves comforter The woods. She sprinted toward the woods, dropping her bag and jumping into her wolf form. Her wolf was amazing, white coat elegant as she is and black socks.

I felt a lump build in my throat, How could I let something so beautiful slip through my fingers?

It is not to late my friend... my wolf said feeling hyper now, as he thought of his mate next to him. I raised my hand signalling the teacher I wanted to leave, of course he had to comply because I was indeed the alphas son and future leader of the pack. I got up racing down the halls at a leasurly jog following my mates scent.

I followed it till I reached the bag she dropped, I slowly stripped and jumped into my wolf form grabbing her bag and my clothes then took off into a sprint following her scent in the twist and turns of the woods.

she was close by, by now. I could feel her presence close by, I then saw her.

She stood in a bra and underwear on a cliff not far from the woods looking down at the water, she looked as if she was going to jump.

My wolf screamed at me and lunged me forward, not caring to think before going. He jumped toward her and grabbed her by the arm pulling her to us and holding her tight, I now seen she had been crying her eyes stained with white streaks, she looked up at us in shock then whimpered her lower lip trembling and she did something I thought she wouldn't do, she hugged us around the neck trembling with sobs.

"Why do you not want us" she sobbed out burying her face into my black fur "Why didn't you just kill me while you were at it" that retched my heart right out of my chest, she was in deep pain and I think I couldn't help her. Of course we still held her close, my huge wolfy head rapping around her small body in an embrace showing we could comfort her.

"Please don't reject me, Please" she sobbed out hiccuping lightly, this broke my heart the most, I gave her the idea that I was rejecting her but I loved her so much, because she was my mate.

my wolf was right I was being selfish, and we'd protect her no matter what. She finally stopped crying long enough to say "I'm sorry I cried on your fur, you probably find this pathetic" she said getting up out of my paws. I felt my wolf awaken inside and whine at her to come back.

she looked back at me frowning "you don't want me, don't beg" she said walking toward the ledge and sitting on it letting her legs hang off the edge "Todays my birthday by the way, if you didn't know" she said looking down.

That was it for me, I ran down the hill grabbing my pants changing into them then walking up the hill again "I never said I rejected you" I said growling and putting my shirt over her head as she put her arms through the sleeves "I loved you for so long" I said sitting down and wrapping my arms around her waste putting my face in her neck breathing in and out trying to calm myself down. I could feel hot tears trickle down her face "You're a monster, making me think you never wanted me" she whispered then she got up from my lap where she sat, "Thanks for the shirt but no thanks, my wolf's silent because of you, she's in pain because of you" she said grabbing her bag and making her way down the hill.

that's when I realized how much I hurt her. Her wolf was silent which meant the bond between human and wolf is broken....meaning the wolf must have gotten really hurt to do this.

I felt beyond terrible.... I felt like the big bad wolf stealing my lil reds innocence.

Chapter 3

I lay in my bed the next day, I told my mom about Samuel and my wolf going silent. She said I could stay home the next day. I laid around the house, crying once in a while.

In the afternoon my brother came into the room, with his mate. When he saw my tears his eyes softened and whispered into his mates ear signalling for her to go "What's wrong?" he asked going over to my bed laying back bringing me into his brotherly embrace.

I began to sob harder than I was before "I think....I got...rejected?" I hiccupped looking at Jeremy feeling my heart ache "My wolf is silent" I buried my face into his chest, like I did when I was a little girl. Jeremy wrapped his arms around my waste kissing my head "Who is the jerk face?" he asked looking down at me.

"Samuel Cliff" I said frowning at how I felt my heart skip a beat at his name "He gave me a note telling me I was pathetic, and that I was nothing a Alpha would want...and...and when I was going to..." I paused looking down "When I was going to jump off Luwaya Cliff he found me dragging me back and telling me he loved me...." I said closing my eyes and burrying my face into his chest again knowing he was probably mad at me for almost jumping.

"Oh Lilli" he said kissing my head again tightening his grip on me "You shouldn't be doing that crap" he said grabbing my chin so I was looking at him "Cause there's more people than just Samuel Cliff who can love you, like me, mom, dad and even Steph" he said smiling down at me "So don't frett my pet, for he'll come scrambling back" he said then sat up with me.

"Thanks Jer" I said kissing his cheek then getting up from the bed "i'm going say hi to steph than go for a run" I said going out of my bedroom seeing a worried Stephanie on the other side "Oh honey, I kinda heard everything" she said bringing me into a hug "I'm so sorry" she said kissing my head.

This is what I loved about Stephanie, she was so loving and compassionate and loved everyone she came to know. She was the perfect mate for Jeremy.

"Yeah I guess so" I said kissing her cheek "I'm going to go for a run" I said making my way past her "Hey we got some good news tonight so be back around 8" she hollered as I made my way barefooted out the door, making my way to the woods where I stripped and jumped into my wolf.

I took off not caring about the branches that hit me or when I fumbled on a tree's root I just wanted to run. After a while of running I smelt a familiar sweet smell, the smell reminded me of warm cookies and woods, then I saw him. Samuel ran around a little patch of yard in wolf form after a smaller wolf, he ran after the little wolf pouncing and playing.

I laid down in the thicket watching the two then the little wolf growled sniffing at the air and growled once more it's eyes pointing towered where I sat, I slowly backed away but Samuel already smelled me I could see how his body stiffened, he walked over to the smaller wolf and nuzzled her neck affectionately, which probably signalled her to change and go inside because that's exactly what she did.

she looked about 5-8 years old with the same dark brown hair that went long down her back, she had the same blue eyes also. I finally noticed Samuel had changed wearing a pair of black shorts "Isabelle, go in tell mom and dad i'm going for a little run" he said kissing her head, she nodded walking into the huge house. He made his way towered where I sat almost cowering "You know? hiding won't help with the fact we're mates" he said now seeing me probably because my coat was an icey white. "You can come out now Liv" he said crossing his arms over his toned chest.

I whined making my way out of the thicket to where he stood, I crawled on my stomach showing he had dominance over me, since he was an alpha and he could kill me in one smack of his paw if he wanted to. He saw me cower and shook his head walking over to me, sitting on his knees "You know, I wrote that note because I thought I would be putting you in danger, since I am an alpha and all" he said crawling closer to me reaching his hand out.

I whined my wolfy whine and crawled closer to him so his hand was on my muzzle. He lightly petted my muzzle making me pur "You're such a beautiful wolf I wish I hadn't hurt you" he sad kissing my muzzle lightly.

I whined agreeing, my wolf was in fact still with me but we were still hurt. I crawled over closer to him and put my head on his lap letting him pet me. I allowed the feeling of love a care come into my heart and I let the thought of him loving me come in as well.

he kissed my muzzle "If you let me, i'll protect you and love you like I should of from the start?" he said looking at me with his clear blue eyes "So if you'll let me? will you be my Mate" he asked petting my head affectionately.

I thought about it and nodded my wolfy head licking his cheek as a signal of me saying yes. He smiled brightly and kissed my muzzle again "You wanna go for a run with me?" he asked standing up.

I nodded my head standing up on all fours feeling playful as I jumped around in circles waiting for him to change. When he did though my breath hitched in my throat as I seen him, his wolf was atleast a foot taller than me, making me want to cower. But then again I was proud because he finally accepted me officially as his mate.

He signalled me to follow him, making his way into the woods taking off into a sprint. Halfway through the run, all four of my paws were aching. Samuel was fast and I couldn't keep up, I laid down at one point on a patch of moss breathing in deeply.

Samuel finally noticed and turned back around making his way toured me Are you okay? He asked in the mind like touching his nose to my Muzzle in a loving manner.

I nodded and licked his muzzle I'm okay you're just really fast I panted leaning against him. He smiled a wolfy smile and walked with me, then lets walk he said walking out onto a cliff, to be exact the cliff I was on the other day. I frowned remembering everything that went on that day.

Samuel saw me frowned and nuzzled my neck purring making sparks build in that one spot. Wanna just sit here and talk? you know face to face instead of in wolf form? If I was in human form I would've blushed, cause I didn't have any clothes.

He must of felt my embarresment cause he made his way down the cliff holding up two bundles of clothing they're both mine, but they'll make due I smiled and grabbed one of the packs from him making my way behind a tree changing then getting dressed. Once I was done I made my way out onto the cliff seeing Samuel sitting on the edge looking at the now pink sky. I walked over and sat down next to him looking at the lake "I think this is good and bad for me" I said honestly looking down at my hands. "Why?" he asked looking at me now making me feel anxious.

"Cause, I feel rejected but now I feel loved...and my brother just got back from Alaska so that's on me too" I said leaning back on my hands. He looked at my hands and nodded "I get it, but I need a luna to be an Alpha without a luna I'm just a simple mutt" he said shrugging his shoulders.

I think he didn't realize what that sentence meant to me because I got straight up and made my way down the hill quickly stripping out of his clothes "Wait! Oliva where are you going"? he hollered making his way towered me.

I turned around still in his shirt "I'm stupid to take you back?? you'll be a simple mutt?? do you know how much that hurts or makes me feel"?! I yelled turning back around huffing and puffing. I walked into the woods not caring where I was going.

All I cared about was getting away from this jerk, that just reched my heart out once more and put my wolf to silence once more.

I got back home around 10 O'clock cause I couldn't find my way back. Everyone was asleep of course except for Jeremy who was sitting on the couch looking at the Tv blankly "Come here" he said opening his arms up. He always knew when I felt terible, that was the best thing about him as a brother.

For once I didn't cry, I didn't complain I just sat in my brothers arms till I fell into a deep sleep where I wish I had to stay cause I had school the next day.

Chapter 4

This was one of those days where you never wanted to get up, because you didn't want to see that one person who could make your heart race.

I got up from bed after 10 minutes of contemplating about if I should fake being sick or just going to school. After a while I decided to go to school, because I'm a nerd and don't want to be late. Walking into my closet I pulled on a pair of black sweats and a baggy sweatshirt not feeling like dressing up today.

When I was done I walked downstairs feeling like crap because of yesterday, but as soon as I got to the bottom of the stairs I was tackled in a hug "Oh my god, where were you yesterday missy"? Stephanie asked hugging me closer into her giant boobs I swear I got hit with a car airbag. I frowned remembering what happened yesterday "Stephanie?" I asked quietly, as I felt one silent tear fall down my cheek "yes?" she said petting my hair "My heart hurts" I said as more tears fell down my cheeks.

She grabbed my chin looking down at me and kissing my cheek "I know it hurts now, but you both with come back around.. I mean you were put together as mates, right?" she said kissing my head and letting me go, "I think you'll be just fine sweetie, and if you want to cut school after a couple classes i'll bail you out to go shopping or something" she said softly giving me one last hug "I hope you'll make through the day though" she said smiling and making her way to the kitchen.

I nodded walking to grab my bag and grab my ugg boots slipping them on "See ya guys"! I yelled walking out of the house.

Walking to the school was a mile walk at least, but I didn't care being a wolf walking never tired me out as much as it did when I was human. Getting to school I went to my locker making sure I had everything then I went to my first class.

I sat down in my seat not caring that Samuel was gone from his seat or that I wasn't taking notes, my heart hurt to much to do anything. All of a sudden while in deep thought I heard the door slam and saw Samuel walk in his eyes red and puffy. I averted my gaze to my hands feeling my heart clench.

I felt a tap on my shoulder, looking back I saw Melany the nerd of the class she held up a note "From Samuel" she whispered throwing the note onto my desk going back to her notes. I was afraid to open the note because the last time I opened a note I ended up running out of the school crying, I grabbed the note opening the edges then reading it slowly.

Dear Olivia.

I cried a lot last night, knowing that I hurt you again emotionally...When I went over the conversation I felt terrible because I sounded like a jerk...I never meant to make it sound like that and I'm sorry... I hope you'll forgive me again, and I hope that we can get to know eachother better.

Please write back or talk to me after class Love Samuel.

I felt my heart flutter and I flipped the paper over taking out a pen

I'll accept your apology, but if you hurt me again I swear I won't hesitate in rejecting an alpha as a mate...I've been un-mated and un-loved for this long, it won't hurt to be again.

Olivia

I handed the note back to Melany and told her to give it to Samuel, He opened the note his face becoming sad and a tear going down his face, he looked up at me catching my eyes and nodded understanding.After and hour of class I got up to walk out but Samuel grabbed my arm "Liv?" I looked back at him, his face looking sad. "Can I ask you something?" I looked at him feeling hesitant but nodded "Yeah?"

"To get to know eachother, would you go out on a date with me"? he asked looking terribly nervous. I frowned at this and then looked around the empty classroom "Time and Place?" I asked my voice sounding sad.

his face perked up "Ummm tomorrow night at 8 and it's a surprise" he said smiling deviously "Wear something really nice" he said then he kissed my cheek walking out of the room. I smiled lightly and touched my cheek, feeling happy that he was actually taking me out. Yet I knew he'd probably hurt me a tiny bit and in reality I never want to reject Samuel.. I knew what parcial rejection felt like and it hurt.

the rest of the day went by slowly, I saw Samuel twice after first hour and one of the times he tried to sit by me at lunch but I wouldn't allow it because I knew he truly loved me as a mate, or at least his wolf loved us more than him...but I think Samuel the man didn't like us at all....

This whole thought went through my head the whole day, making me almost depressed but when I got home and took off to the woods, I felt no pain. No sorrow. Just trees ripping at my fur and my paws slapping against the ground.

Running was my wolfs comfort, and now that she wasn't as silent as she was 3 days ago, she felt free.

I ran to the ledge where me and Samuel sat yesterday and laid down on the ledge, taking a deep breath I closed my eyes hoping to rest them but instead I fell into a black Sleep of nothing.

Chapter 5

Wolf howls woke me from my slumber, I opened my eyes to see I was on a ledge. I looked around and calmed down seeing I was still on the ledge where I had fallen asleep earliar but that was the thing? It was night time? and stars were out. It wasn't night when I had came out.

"We found her"! I heard someone yell, that's when I noticed I was in human form....Clothed?

my dad ran up the cliff toured me and smacked into my small body "Olivia! oh my baby girl! you're alright" he crushed me into his chest holding me tight "Where have you been young lady?" he asked letting go of me finally "If it wasn't for Samuel, we wouldn't have found you" he said which made my heart break even more, because it made me remember why I was out here in the first place.

"Daddy, our wolves love eachother more than our humans" I said hugging him once more "I'm sorry I worried you daddy, but I can't take it anymor e....I can't take the thought of him not loving me besides his wolf" I started to sob into my fathers chest.

He sighed softly kissing my head and rubbing my back lightly "It's gunna be okay honey" he said starting to walk backwords "You want a piggy back, back to the car?" he asked me as we walked halway down the hill.

I nodded as he turned around, I hopped onto his back wrapping my arms around his neck like I did when I was a kid, and laid my head on his shoulder letting my tears fall silently, I closed my wet eyes letting darkness surround me with the sounds of sirens in the background.

****

Samuels P.O.V

I and my wolf were in a frenzy, My mates father and mother came by my house, my little sister answering the door to find out my mate was missing. When I found this out I headed out the door stripping and throwing myself into the air turning into my wolf sniffing the air for her.

I went to all the places we had been yesterday, but nowhere was she. Then I went to our ledge seeing her tiny body lying there in human form. I averted my eyes away from her naked body grabbing a bundle of my clothes from behind a rotten log.

I turned into my human form pulling on a pair of pants then walking over to my mates limp body putting my black shirt on then the black pants. I kissed her head making her whine in her sleep, then I made my way down the cliff again going to tell her dad I had found her but didn't want to bring her because if he was the one to wake her up, she'd have a fit and probably hate him more then he felt she already did.

It hurt to know she probably hated him for not feeling the exact same way she did, he loved her but then again not as much as his wolf did. Maybe after he was fully mated with her? or when he would mark her he could return her love? these questions haunted him till he got back to his house where Olivia's mother sat with her husband and my parents talking to eachother.

My parents looked angry "So you found your mate son? and rejected her?" my father almost yelled standing up but was stopped by my mother who put her hand in my fathers standing up "Eddy I think he could have a reason" she said kissing his cheek "First we need to find the poor girl" she smiled at me and walked over hugging me "Did you find her my darling?" she asked kissing my cheek "Did you find your mate?"

I frowned at her saying that but nodded "Shes at the cliff above Leeway Lake, I dressed her because she had shifted into her human form...I didn't think I should of carried her back because I think she hates me..." I said feeling ashamed that I didn't do the simple thing of bringing my mate back to her family.

My father stood up and went up to me patting my shoulder "The least you did was find her son, I don't blame you" he said then made his way out of the house. Olivia's mother then came towered me "Samuel, she loves you..I hope you know that and it's killing her in the inside not knowing whether your feelings for her are true or not, but I hope you make a good descision for yourself and your mate" she said kissing my cheek and making her way out of the house.

My father stood glaring at me while my mother smiled her loving smile "Samuel, go tuck in Lillian then go off to bed," dad said crossing his arms against his chest. I nodded "Yes sir" then made my way upstairs to my little sister Lillie's room, where she laid looking at the doorway where I entered.

I entered the pink room feeling happiness overwelm me "Hi Munchkin" I said walking towered her bed where she crawled around on to get to where I sat down. "Hi Sammy!" she giggled out happily hugging my huge frame with her small arms.

"Moma and Dad said you gotta go to bed now" I said kissing my sisters dark head, She nodded crawling across her huge bed, then under the covers where she seemed so small.

I got up walking over to her kissing her head "Night" I said walking towered the doorway "Night Sammy" she said grabbing her stuffed gray wolf and snuggling into the covers. I loved my sister, as much as I loved Olivia, Well at least as much as I should love Olivia. I stopped in the middle of the hallway, my heart hurt. Like internally it hurt like heck.

I walked to my bedroom stripping down to my boxers and getting into bed thinking of my Olivia out there without me, on our cliff probably thinking he didn't love her when he loved her like nothing else.

That's the last thing he thought before his lids slid down, and he was surrounded by darkness.

Chapter 6

O livia;

I woke up in the morning with the light coming through my shades blinding me.

"God" I mumbled groggily sitting up to see my curtains were wide open? standing up I looked around then walked to the curtains pulling them closed before I stretched adjusting to the darkened light of the room.

Walking over to the bathroom I looked at myself in the mirror, seeing the same girl with blue eyes and black hair, but my eyes were sadly red rimmed and blood shot "Great" I said bending over and splashing my face with water then looking up at the image in the mirror, seeing the red lines slowly disappear.

I walked out of the bathroom, going to my closet I grabbed a pair of sweatpants and a tank top then I made my way downstairs.

I came to a stop at the last step seeing a face I never expected to see ever....Samuel was standing in the middle of my living room with a rose in hand "Olivia" he said smiling.

Looking into the kitchen I saw my mom with a huge smiled on her face, cooking food "Mom you let Him in"? I asked adding emphasis on Him, mom shrugged finishing her pancakes. Turning to him I was smirking devilishly and went over to the stack of pancakes grabbing the biggest one.

I smirked walking closer to him then slapped him...with the pancake, I went back to the kitchen setting the pancake back on the counter. Crossing my arms over my chest I turned to look over at his dumbfounded face.

"Why in the heck did you just slap me with a pancake?" he asked raising an eyebrow at me, rubbing his cheek with his hand.

I smirked and stepped forward "Because you're a jerk, you hurt me really bad, right here" I pointed to my heart and frowned "I'm going to make you beg for me to be you're full mate cause you're a terrible mate rejecting me, then telling me you love me...I almost killed myself because of you! I will not be a door mat for you to walk all over" I said growling, I looked over at my mom, to see Jeremy was now there looking proud as ever.

I looked over at Samuel looking down at the ground "Right now, get out of my house and don't come back till you feel i'm calmed down" I said not wanting to see him at this point. Looking at him I saw a tear go down his cheek "I'm sorry for hurting you Olivia" he walked over to me setting the rose on the counter then kissing me on the cheek "I'll be back when you want me too, I hope you can forgive me for being a terrible excuse for a mate."

I was looking at the ground the whole time, but I saw his black biker boots making their way away from me out the door where I heard it close silently.

That's where I broke down, I felt a deep pain In my chest that hurt me so bad I fell to the ground clenching my chest then I felt tears coming down my face.

"Jeremy bring her to the couch" I heard my mom say as I felt a pair of arms wrap around my chest, lifting me up and bringing me over to the couch and sitting me down on his lap.

I curled up and pulled my knees to my chest "Jer....my chest hurts" he nodded wrapping his arms around my small body "I know"

I burried my face in his chest and started to cry "I hurt him really bad Jeremy, hurting him is hurting me more" I cried feeling terrible. Jeremy rubbed circles in my back soothingly then kissed my head "I know but he needs to know where you guys stand and that he did hurt you...He needs to feel that pain honey, so it's okay"

I sniffled and looked up at him nodding, then I started to get up,"I think i'm going to take a walk in human form" I said walking toward the door, putting my hightops on before making my way onto our front yard where I ran toward the woods.

I ran as fast as I can tears flowing down my cheeks. My chest hurts so much, along with my heart. "Samuel i'm sorry" I whispered to no one in particular, before I stopped running, or stopped moving and just stopped in the middle of the woods, my tears still flowing freely.

I fell to the ground sobbing, pulling my knees to my chest I kept crying not caring that this was the woods, and an enemy pack was still here.

"well hello there little wolf" I heard from behind me, I turned then to see the alpha I crossed paths with a few days ago, I frowned up at him then stood. "Hello Alpha" I said curtsying to show that I meant no harm.

"No need for that little wolf, why the tears all of a sudden" He asked putting his hand beneath my eyes to remove the tears that were there. "Did you get hurt little one?" He asked touching my arms in a comforting manner.

I just nodded, not wanting to speak for I was afraid i'd break down in front of this Alpha for I broke down in front of Samuel.

"By who?" he then asked "Your mate?" he frowned and put an arm around me once I nodded my head and took a deep breath.

"Well, Little wolf, would you like to come home with me so you could get cleaned up and get some food in ya?" he asked looking down at me, smiling as warmly as he could. An Alphas hospitallity shouldn't be denied so I just nodded and let him drag me out of the forrest, into the unknown.

Chapter 7

M e and Alpha David made our way to a huge pack house, when I entered the house I noticed a lot of people like 15 of them in the living room and 6 in the kitchen.

"I hope you don't mind being squished, this is how this is all the time" he said walking toward the kitchen where a pregnant woman stood, leaning against the counter talking to someone who looked to be her mate.

The man who was the girls mate stood when he saw David enter "Alpha, who is this"? he asked as looked at me, then the women's eyes followed his widening and she smiled widely.

"You look exactly like Jeremy" she said getting up slowly then walking toward me,wrapping her arms around me "you must be Olivia" I smiled hugging back, feeling her stomach pressing against mine.

"My name's Melissa, and this is my Mate Jamie, we knew your brother Jeremy" Melissa smiled and kissed my cheek. "It's nice to meet you also" I said unsure of myself, because Jeremy hadn't mentioned them before.

David came behind me and smiled "It's alright, Olivia" he patted me on the back then led me to the fridge "Want something to drink, water, juice, milk?"

I shook my head "Um I'm okay" I smiled reassuring him, he shut the fridge and made his way to the dining room where he pulled a chair back "Why don't you sit here Olivia" smiling I walked over and sat down as David pushed in my seat, I looked at the house then, how big it was, but comparing to Sam's house it was small.

thinking of Samuel I sighed deeply "Are you okay Olivia"? David asked, sitting in the chair next to me putting a plate toppled with pancakes in front of me."Um yes, I'm...fine" then I realized how un-fine I was because right then my heart felt like it was going to retch out of my chest.

Tears starting falling down my cheeks in waterfalls then I sobbed, I seen David through the blur and saw him walk out of the room, probably giving me space.

After what seemed like forever he finally came back, when I was still crying and someone stood next to him, someone I smelt a mile away, someone who I loved with all the broken pieces of my heart.

Samuel...

I choked out a sob, and averted my eyes feeling like I was a shameful mate to him, I saw a pair of black biker boots before I felt myself being scooped into a pair of arms.

"I'll take her back to my house" Samuel said then I felt myself being carried out of the house, I still cried until I was silent, limp in his arms. I caught him looking at me every once in a while, but he said nothing probably thinking i'd break.

After about 20 minutes he walked into his house with me still in his arms, he walked upstairs where I was put on a bed, his bed to be exact. Then he did the thing I wouldn't expect him to do, he sat next to me, pulling me into his lap, he wrapped his arms around my waste and kissed my cheek "I'm so sorry Olivia" he hugged me closer and I sat there silent just wanting to feel the warmth of my mate.

I took a deep breath before looking up at Samuel "Why are you here?" I asked laying my head on his chest to weak to get up. He looked down at me one single tear running down his cheek "Because I love you and feel really bad about hurting you." another tear went down his cheek and he burried his face in my neck "Please forgive me Olivia, it hurts being away from you, it hurts to see you hurting please just forgive me" he begged, I felt more tears going onto my shoulder soaking into my shirt.

I felt my heart beat a little bit faster and I felt like I was going to cry myself, but I just couldn't find myself to do it, I turned myself so I was facing him on his lap and wrapped my arms around his neck holding him close as he cried as hard as I did just a few seconds ago.

I held him till we both were laying on the bed with him laying against me with his head on my chest "Do you forgive me?" he asked his voice cracking a little.

I smiled and looked at him, his eyes where red looking up at me "I forgive you" I said then kissed him lightly. He kissed back then pulled back looking into my eyes "I love you Olivia"

I smiled and thought of this for a while then said "I love you too" Samuel smiled the biggest smile then kissed me again not pulling back this time, when we came up for air we both just sat there looking up at the ceiling.

"Do you think that you would move into the pack house?" Sam asked after a while. The question startled me because I didn't really thought of that till now. When an alpha or any male find their mate the female has to move into the pack house with them.

"Um...I never really put any thought to it" I said honestly looking up at the ceiling awkwardly.

Samuel sat up all of a sudden looking at me "And were you thinking of not moving into the pack house"? he asked looking at me with a look of concern. I shrugged and pulled my legs up to my chest "I never really thought of it till now Samuel" I said now feeling uncomfortable about the question.

I mean it was true, most mates want nothing but to be together forever but ever since Samuel hurt me one part of my heart/my wolf wanted nothing more than to be away from him.

I must have went silent because Samuel was shaking my shoulder with a concerned look on his face "Olivia? are you okay." I nodded smiling "I'm fine it's just I think me and myself are not ready for the life your wolf and your being an alpha will bring us." I looked up at him and saw more tears rolling down his face.

"So you don't want to be my mate is that it? this is your revenge on me isn't it to make me beg and plead for you to live with me and be mine cause I will do it, I'll get on my knees right now!?" he started to sound angry, that one simple wolf, his mate could make him cry, an alpha.

"Nooo you didn't let me finish" I put my hand on his shoulder "we're not ready for this life....but i'm willing to try so we don't have to hurt every single day without you." I saw his smile come back and he picked me up off the bed swinging me around the room.

"Oh thank god!" he yelled and kissed me on the lips then set me down "Thank you for believing in us" he whispered bending so he could put his forehead on mine.

"And thank you for believing in me as your mate" he smiled into my eyes and kissed me one last time "We should go to your house and pack your things?" he asked and I nodded intwining my fingers into his as he pulled me out of the room down the stairs and out the door.

my new life was about to start.

Chapter 8

I walked into my house, hand in hand with Samuel.

Jeremy sat with Stephanie in his lap "So I guess ya'll back together again?" he smiled wrapping his arms around Stephanies waste.

"Well of course they are, they're forever mates anyways" my mother chimed in coming out of the kitchen with cookies on a tray, she set them on the counter then looked over at me smiling almost enchantedly "My little girl finally has a man." she looked as if she was going to cry, but no tears hit her cheeks, for my father came through the door in a huff.

"You seriously have the guts to step a foot into this household?" he pointed a bony finger scutinizing Samuel, "After you hurt my daughter the way you did?" he took a deep breath "I don't care if you're mates, I am not allowing this man anywhere near this house or my daughter." his face was red showing all anger radiating off him.

But what made me worry twice as much was that I felt Samuel shaking next to me, that's the worst thing you could ever do is keep mates from eachother, Samuel was going into protection mode and he did't care who he had to go through to protect what he was protecting, which in this case was me.

He started shaking and his skin was almost red hot, "Please dad go upstairs so he'll calm down" I said calmly putting myself in front of Samuel to calm him down, but nothing was going to work for this wolf of mine, he wasn't in control anymore and I was only in it's way from killing my old man.

I held my ground though like my father was behind me "I'm not letting this guy take me in my own home, I'm standing my ground" he stood his arms at his sides in a fighting mode, I opened my mouth to say something but it never got out before I was knocked to the ground something on top of me, I looked up to see Samuels wolf in a protective stance with me between his front legs and his mouth snarling and snapping at my father.

I rolled onto my stomach but I felt his paw press onto my back keeping me down, which let me tell you his paws were huge and he was strong.

I whimpered as I tried to push his paw off, his head bowed down licking my cheek before he continued his growling, I looked up at my father who wasn't shaking because of years of practice changing, he simply stood waiting for the right moment to spring into action.

Samuel growled one last time then he pushed himself forward toward my father, who finally sprung into his wolf form which was gray with white paws.

They went after each other snapping and biting, I was so focused on the fight when someone touched my back, I winced as I looked back at my mom, who looked at me in horror as she held up her red hands "Oh my darling, you're hurt" she said going to the kitchen to grab a washcloth and wetting it with warm water.

I tried to sit up but failed cause of the pain, arms around around my from pulling me off the ground and into a bar stool. "Oh baby sis let me see your back sweetie" Jeremy said rubbing my arms soothingly "It looks pretty bad" he kissed my forehead "I'm going to go and try to get the guys away from eachother" he smiled and walked out the front door going after the two men who hurt me physically and emotionally.

my mom slowly rubbed at the wounds as Stephanie held my hand seeing the pain in my eyes, it hurt really bad, if only Samuel removed his paw from my back before he went after my father. I winced as the wounds stung then touched my moms hand to let her know to stop "I'm going to go find them and stop this" I got up slowly trying not to hurt myself.

I walked out the front door trying to sniff the guys out but I found nothing, I walked deeper into the woods sniffing as I went but then I smelt something, but it smelt like dirt and dried blood. I covered my nose as I got closer to the smell, then I saw the source and I wanted to cry or puke.

A dead wolf lay his eyes rolled behind his head, dead.

I dropped to my knees wanting to puke, but then something hit me, was he attacked or died of common things? rolling back onto my feet and stepped closer holding my breath, his throat was ripped out clean I finally seen.

Rogues....

I turned around running as fast as I could "Samuel!" I screamed jumping and leaping wanting to find him, to be safe and to not puke all over the ground. "Samuel!" I screamed once more before I heard scuffling and snapping jaws.

In front of me was Samuel with my father in a death grip by the throat. My mind went back to the dead wolf making me feel sick "Samuel, you let him go right now!" I yelled falling to the ground, as my back burned. "Samuel, please let him go, he meant to protect me. He meant well...You need to help me right now, see you hurt my back and I can't get up" I whimpered tears staining my cheeks for the fear of my fathers death.

Samuels eyes shot toward me but he didn't let go just yet, I turned around showing his the three wounds that were almost healed, he imediatiatly let go of my father who dropped to the ground panting. He got down on his stomach crawling over toward me whining. "It's okay Samuel, but you don't go after my father when i'm underneath you, I don't care if you're ticked off." I said petting his solf fur.

He whined once more licking my cheek and crawling behind me, wrapping his body around my small one. he put his giant head in my lap whining lowly "It's okay, it's not that bad Sam" I put my hand on his head petting him slowly, "It'll heal but you do not go after my father, killing him would have hurt me right here" I put my hand on my heart then continued petting his head.

He let out a growl/whine then stood up grabbing my shirt sleave to try and help me up off the ground. I smiled trying to get off the ground, but saddly failed which ended in me falling back onto the ground.

Samuel gave me a worried look before getting back onto his stomach. He sneezed and pointed at his back with his nose. I smiled crawling over to him and throwing my leg onto the other side of him before climbing on and holding onto his fur.

I looked back at dad who was limping toward me looking at my wounds, he growled and licked my cheek "I'm okay Daddy," I petted his ear before Samuel let out a bark before taking off further into the forest. "Oh god" I just remembered why I first came to him "Samuel, there are rogues!" I yelled because he probably couldn't hear me, if I didn't.

Samuel stopped running and started growling "They're not here right now, I'm just saying I saw a dead body of a wolf on the way here and...and...it had it's throat ripped out" I felt a tear go down my cheek as I buried my face into Sams back.

He growled once more then turned his head touching his wet nose to my cheek telling me it's okay. I buried my face deeper in his thick fur murmering "It was terrible, there was so much blood" I cried, tears making his fur wet.

he was looking at me, his head turned toward me, which was probably painful in his part because his neck was turned in a hurtful position. I lifted my head kissing his muzzle. "It's okay darling, just bring me home so I can get better" I whispered before he took off out of the woods.

When I seen my house in the distance my heart dropped...the house was on fire and my mom stood in the front yard, as we got closer my eyes went wide as I saw a body on the lawn...Blonde hair was now bloody and blue eyes were now white.

Stephanie was dead, and Jeremy was no where to be found......

My brother was missing and my sister in law was dead.....

my heart wreched as I crawled off Samuels back falling into the bloody grass.

Chapter 9

I felt almost numb as I walked through the rubble that used to be our house, all things were burned from our old leather couches to our family portraits, even worste of all Stephanie laid still in the front yard cold and lifeless covered in her own blood.

Last night my dad and Samuel apologized to me once more, then to eachother because I think they realized there was something bigger then the love life of me. Samuel invited us to stay at his house for the night which we reluctently took and I slept in Samuels room with him while my parents got their own room. Samuels parents graciously took us in as if we were family, his mom babying me as if I was her own daughter.

I felt two arms wrap around me, taking me out of my thoughts "Babe you okay?" Samuel asked kissing my shoulder before turning me around in his arms so we were now face to face.

"I just can't believe Stephanies dead, and my house burned to the ground." I whispered before putting my head on his chest "And I don't even know where Jeremy went which is making me worried." looking up at him I seen the love in his eyes.

"Come on, I want to bring you somewhere," he said kissing my nose before grabbing my hand and walking toward the now black doorway. "Where are we going?" I asked as he brought me toward his car that was parked out front, I got into his car noticing he wasn't answering but he was smiling wide "Oh somewhere" I smirked before shaking my head and looking out the window saddly as the charred house passed by as he pulled out of our driveway, getting onto the dirt road.

We sat in a comfortable silence, Samuel held my hand the whole time, as he drove the car into town. I looked around the town seeing people walking in and out of stores. The car stopped all of a sudden in front of a furniture store.

"Why are we here?" I asked as Samuel got out of open my door, I got out as he did and frowned "Why are we here Samuel?" I asked seriously, wanting to know.

"Well you're in my house for the time, so I thought we could buy you a bed, and some stuff for your very own bedroom" he said grabbing my hand and walking me into the store without even waiting for a reply from me.

We walked into the store getting a Welcome to Kiki's furnature and wood. Samuel imediatly went toward the beds dragging me along with him, "So anything you want, you can have, the price is nothing but a number." I frowned but looked around at beds, knowing he won't take No for an answer.

We looked around the store almost all day laying on multiple beds and sitting in many chairs before we were completely done and out of the store.

Samuel never told me the price of the furnature but I was worried it would be like a lot, for all we got. I didn't want to seem like a gold digger, just letting him pay for everything.

When we got back to his house I felt almost drained of all my energy, I went into the house to find out that my parents had called Alpha David to come and get Stephanies body and to bury it, we'd have the funeral in a couple days.

I walked up to Samuels room, kicking off my shoes and taking off my jacket I crawled into bed and wrapped up in the blankets. I hadn't cried in so long it seemed like my eyes would burst, and finally in that moment, they did.

I cried letting out the sobs and tears that were waiting to be let out, for my brother, for my sister in law and for that wolf who had to die for no simple reason. I buried my face into the blankets wanting nothing but to close my eyes and sleep, but afraid of seeing the wolfs deadly stare, turned toward me.

I whimpered curling into a tiny ball pulling my legs to my chest "I wish rogues never existed...." I whispered then felt the bed dip down, and two arms wrap around me, I felt the familiar buzz and knew it was Samuel,"Darling, are you okay?" he asked pulling my arms away from my my legs so he could wrap his arms around me properly.

"No, Samuel i'm not" I whimpered "I mean why wouldn't I be? My brother is god knows where and my sister in law is dead" I cried out grabbing his arms from around me and crawling to the edge of the bed trying to get as far as I could away from him.

"Did I do something to upset you?" He asked sound a little hurt, I felt the hurt in my heart then and rolled over looking at him, conferming the hurt "No you didn't do anything, I just....I just can't lay next to you right now" I said feeling awkward, so I rolled back over and put my feet on the ground.

"We just got furnature for my room, but there's still a bed in there so, while I recover from the dead of my sister in law, i'm going to sleep alone." I said going to the closet to grab a extra pillow and blanket before making my way to the door "Goodnight Samuel" I said before opening the door and closing it behind me, feeling my heart ache.

I walked to the next room opening it to see the room I was introduced to last night, just a couple things changed, like the sheets and blankets were mine and there were a couple things of mine in here.

I walked to the bed putting the extra pillow and blanket down before flipping the blankets over and laying back down, "Jeremy I hope you find your way home" I whispered before closing my eyes and burying my face into the pillows and sheets.

Chapter 10

B lank white eyes glared at me through a film of death, I looked around the body to see the pool of blood that stained the green grass red. I knealed down petting the dead wolfs white fur, I dragged my hand up and down it's body, till it hit the slit between shoulderblade and chin where the wolfs neck was ripped out red blood oozing out, but then I looked closer at the eyes staring back at me. And that's when I noticed the wolf changing into human form. What was staring back at me were Samuels eyes.

He was dead

Someone was grabbing on my hands, I opened my eyes my vision blurred by the tears in them. "Oh my god please don't die." I cried to the person in front of me because my vision was still blurred.

"Shhhh, I'd never let anyone hurt you shhhh" someone whispered rubbing my back where rugged scars lay in 3 virtical lines on my back "I promise" he whispered again kissing my forehead, at this point I knew it was Samuel, he had me in his lap with his arms wrapped around me protectivally.

I blinked my eyes a couple times, blinking the tears out of my eyes before looking up at the man I loved, he was looking down at me with worrisome eyes "Are you okay darling, I heard you screaming and I had to come in" he said kissing my head gently, then kissing my lips as he tightened his grip a little bit in a protective posture.

"I'm fine Samuel, It was just a bad dream." smiling at him I grabbed his arms from around me and got off his lap so I was standing on the ground "I think I just need to get a glass of water" I said sincerely before turning on my feet to go to the door.

"Olivia?" I heard him say, making me stop with my hand on the door knob.

"Yes?" I asked not turning to him, I didn't want to see those eyes again because I knew i'd see those plain old dead ones instead of his bright ones.

"What was your nightmare about?" he asked sounding concerned, "It w as...nothing, it was a simple nightmare Samuel, don't worry about it." I said before twisting the doorknob and making my way down the hall then down the stairs, not waiting for a reply.

Tonight I didn't want to see him or those eyes cause I knew i'd break down if I looked at them or him for to long. I never want to see him dead again. Walking into the kitchen I grabbed a blue mug, grabbing a green tea bag I turned on the faucet filling the cup before putting it into the microwave for two minutes.

Leaning against the counters I started to remember the dream and felt as if I was going to break, but I didn't want to. I turned around to open the microwave that had beeped, I took the cup into my hands which were shaking by now and set it on the counter.

I took the tea bag in my hand before putting it into the water letting the water get darker.

while I waited I leaned against the counters wanting to get the image out of my head but I was saddly failing, I rubbed my eyes then turned around.

I was now face to face with a very sad looking Samuel, and let me tell you, Samuel looked like a lost puppy when he was sad "Olivia, i'm worried about you:" he whispered walking toward me, I was backed up upon the counters my eyes now shut "Did you dream of me?" he asked sounding hurt "Cause I could feel your pain while you slept, it the pain of a mate finding out her mate got killed" he said going a little closer to me "It's the pain, I think that told me exactly what the dream was, you dreamt I died and now you won't look at me because you're afraid you'll dream this forreal? isn't it"

the thing was, he knew me better then I knew myself and it hurt that he knew that.

I opened my eyes looking up at his, "I didn't want to say it" I whimpered before pushing myself off the counter and hugging him, feeling love and comfort radiating off of him.

"babe it'll be alright, I promise you because we're together right now and we will be together, forever. I promise" he wrapped his arms around me and kissing my head. I buried my face into his chest feeling the comfort "Here, put your feet on mine and i'll bring your upstairs" he said kissing head once more.

I did as he said, to tired to argue, I grabbed my tea cup and let him walk with me on him. He did it without seeming the least bit tired. when we got to the top of the stairs he let me down, my tea now cooled.

"Do you still want to sleep alone?" he asked looking down at the floor, as I took a sip of my tea. I looked at him remembering the nightmare and shook my head rapidly "No" before grabbing his bedroom doorknob and opening the door before making my way to my side of the bed putting my tea on the bedside table.

Samuel stood on the other side of the bed ready to shut off the nightlight I got worried and shook my head "Please don't turn it off Sam, Please" I whimpered getting under the covers and pouting at him with my lip puffed out.

He chuckled and left the light on crawling under the covers "Even if the light was on or off I could protect you" he said wrapping his arms around me for the third time tonight burying his face into my neck then closing his eyes seeming content.

"I know, but that's the thing Samuel, you can protect me from everything that is out here or in the dark but the truth is, you can protect me from the things that lurk in the depths of my dreams,I have to face those things alone" I whispered the last part before closing my eyes.

feeling Samuels breath steady on my neck I knew he was almost asleep, but his body was still on full attack mode, ready to attack anything that moved toward me.

I put my hands on his and took a deep breath before letting sleep take over me, hoping for a dreamless sleep.

***

I was awoken by someone moving beside me, I opened my eyes to see no arms around my waste and no warmth next to me, I flipped over to see Samuel standing and stretching next to the bed.

Stretching his arms into the air he yawned and ran his hand through his bedhead making it more ruffled then it already was.

I smiled sitting up pulling my knees to my chest "Why are you up so early?" I asked yawning lightly as I looked at his pajamas that he must've change into last night.

Samuel turned looking at me with his goofy smile and leaned forward going to kiss me but I covered my mouth muffling "morning breath" before glaring at him with my eyes but smiling inside about the smirk he offered as a reply.

he put his knee on the bed leaning further toward me then grabbed my hands pinning them on either side of me before kissing me lightly "I do not care, I want a good morning kiss" he chuckled before standing back up and making his way to the bathroom, "I'm going to take a quick shower, you're going to meet the rest of the pack today" he said before walking into the bathroom and shutting the door.

Wait.....rest of the pack? then it hit me, the only pack member I've ever met are his mom and dad well and Samuel of course, he was the Alpha. But I never had met the pack? and today I was going to meet them? Oh my god, was he going to present me as his luna?

I was freaked out getting up from the bed going to the wardrobe opening it to see my simple clothes, not seeing a introduction to the pack kind of outfit. At this point I would go to Stephanie and Jeremy's room to see if Stephanie had anything.

But saddly she was dead now, and Jeremy was gone....

"It'll be okay" I whispered before grabbing a red summer dress from a party last year at the beach. The dress was knee length, heart neckline and straps that could come off so it could be strapless.Slipping it on, it hugged my curves perfectly, fitting me perfectly.

"You look perfect" I heard behind me, I looked into the mirror I was looking into, seeing the reflection of Samuel with just a towel on, looking back at me.

I smiled back at him "Well I'd hope you'd say that," I said before putting my hair up in a messy bun

"I mean if you're going to present me as the luna or your mate officialy, I must look the part right?" I replied starting to figit with my hands as I got even more nervous then before.

Samuel facial expression softened and he moved forward kissing me lightly "yes, I am introducing you as the luna today, and there's no part to look like cause as luna it's all about being yourself, and you're beautiful in all you wear, so i'm not worried" he kissed my cheek before rubbing it with his thumb then making his way to his wardrobe.

I turned around quickly while he changed then when he was finished he tapped my shoulder "Well we better go before everyone comes up here wondering what I did with their daughter" he said grabbing my hand and going to the door, opening it then walking out.

I was going to be presented as the Luna today. One question in particular was bugging me though and that was.

would I be a good leader?

Chapter 11

S amuel and I made our way into the woods, he explained to me that there was a pack house that was for the pack. I didn't see why his home wasn't the pack house? it was big enough.

But I didn't question, just followed as we got further into the woods my breathing got labored and I had to take a couple breaks, which only made Samuel more worried for me, I didn't know why.

"Why are you...so worried about me?" I asked at my third break.

Samuel stopped and looked at me saddly "Because I hurt you, and I don't want you to get hurt again" he said simply taking out a waterbottle and handing me it. I grabbed it taking a couple gulps before handing it back to him.

I started walking again, starting to hear some voices in the distance, then I saw it. A huge house stood with people in the yard talking and playing yard games. "Oh my god, there's so many people" I said frowning, then looking back at Samuel who came walking through the bushes behind me.

He chuckled grabbing my hand, and walking toward the house. I followed close behind looking as people froze and looked at us, some gazes with curiosity, some with total jealousy.

Then as we came closer to the house I saw Sam's parents standing on the porch "Oh Olivia, you look so beautiful" Sams mom said rushing over to me and giving me a bear hug, which was saying a lot since we're werewolves.

I hugged back though cause I didn't want to seem rude, Samuels dad smiled at me giving me a small hug, not as long as his mom.

I was glad I'm a hugger, cause the hugging continued throughout the pack. meeting so many people, I was surprised I even remembered any of their names? But Sam of course helped me throughout the process.

****

<<Sams Point of View.>>

My beautiful mate made her way around the pack, I watched close behind her. Helping her with names and introductions.

Being the future Alpha, she was going to be my Luna and I hoped everyone would except her, at least not like I did, I rejected/excepted her, and this tore me apart right down to my core. My wolf went silent those 4 days of hell, we both went through.

I watched as she made her way through the yard into the house, she met my future Beta Luke, and third in command Kyle including their mates Larissa and Jennifer.

most of them are from our school, she got hugs, kisses on the cheek (which I didn't like) and bows and curtsies from all pack members.

I loved how she had the Luna feel, that most of the members wanted to be around her, except the pack whores, who were probably jealous because of my beautiful mate.

I grabbed onto her, wrapping my arm around her waste and kissing her cheek, tonight I was going to officially announce my alpha title and Olivia at my side as Luna.

I now noticed my dad was on the deck holding one hand up to signal everyone to stop, Olivia looked at me then smiled and watched as everyone silenced "Welcome everyone to my sons official coming out party, as Alpha and leader to the pack, I'd like to thank everyone for coming and I hope you all have a great night, now your new Alpha shall say a couple of words, then dinner will be served." I smiled at this, my father. The Alpha excepting that I was indeed the alpha.

I walked up to the deck/stage looking down at all my pack mates, then I looked down at my Mate standing next to my parents, looking as if she were the part of the family already.

"Welcome everyone, I would like to thank my father for the amazing intro-duction, but now I would like to say a couple things." I paused looking at everyone then Olivia, winking at her before continuing "I'd like to say first off, that becoming your Alpha is an amazing honor and I am going to take this seriously like my father did. I will stand by each and every one of you whether in battle or hunting, I will stand by you. As well as me, my mate, your new Luna will also stand by you, in finding her way emotionally and physically as your Luna. My friends and Family, I'm honored to be your Alpha. Thank you." I smiled as everyone applauded.

I walked off the stage, to where Olivia and my parents were all beaming with joy. Though looking at Olivia, she seemed almost nervous. "you okay babe?" I asked going behind her, wrapping my arms around her waist and kissing her shoulder.

She looked at me smiling and nodded "I'm fine, that was an amazing speach by the way."

I smiled at her, as the plates of food were being grabbed and people sat everywhere on the grass, and tables.

****

Mystery's P.o.v.

Breathing hard I let the body of the deer drop, my fangs sliding back into the skin that now tingled. Pulling my sleeve a bit I wiped my mouth with the back of my hand.

I had been traveling for a while now and had happened upon a deer running in the woods. I spotted it with my amazing eyesight and now it lay dead upon the ground. I growled now crouching upon the ground as I smelt something...Something almost sweet but ferrel.

I started to run, feeling the power rise up in me as I did. I looked around me seeing the forrest fly by me. I was halfway through the forest when I smelt the most enticing smell in all my years of living, I came upon a opening in the trees, showing a house with a bunch of people, or should I say a bunch of werewolves.

But in the middle of them stood the most beautiful girl in all my existence. She stood at least 5'4 with brown hair that was straight at the moment with the most beautiful blue eyes ever.

I wanted to know this she-wolf so bad, but then I saw the man next to her, hugging and kissing this girl with such passion.

She had a Mate? I put my head down looking down at the ground, feeling my undead heart break. I have been looking for almost 4 millenia to find my mate. Whether Vampire, werewolf or human. I wanted a mate.

To live forever alone in a world full of mates, it hurts so much.

I sat in the leaves feeling my heart hurt, painfully and slowly. I just couldn't believe she had a mate. After this much time why did she have to have a mate?

Leaning against the tree behind me, I took a deep breath looking up at the deep blue sky, I then stood up noticing a couple of the mutts put their noses to the air and whining.

I guess to Werewolves, Vampires smelt utterly sweet, like the sickening sweet that would make you wanna puke your gutts up, but that was the thing. I'm used to it.

starting to back up I watched as the beautiful girl turned her head, probably feeling the tenseness of the pack around her.

I backed up into the thicket then started running hearing a bunch of running paws behind me.

They were doing a perimeter check, and they were going to find me, because I wanted my mate officially.

I stopped and slowed down bending down and grabbing a rock then slicing it across my arm and head, I laid down on the ground slowing down my breathing so it seemed almost human like. then waited as men and wolves came running toward me. Now is the time to act.

"Oh....god did you see it, it came out of no where a man with sharp teeth, he sliced me up." I cried putting pressure on the cuts.

I growled at the stinging pain then looked up at the men.

one man, who looked like my mates, mat walked toward me "Are you okay? what is your name?"

Before I 'blacked out' I looked up at the guy "Jack" before 'passing out.'

chapter 12

Olivia's P.o.v

You know i'd never had expected my new pack to be carrying a body back with them. Or at least not one they found in the woods.

I sat in the pack house waiting for Samuel to get back from the pack hospital which I guess was in another part of the woods. I was nervouse, I felt something wrong about the 'human' they brought in.

I could smell that he was different from humans but I couldn't place the smell, it was almost sickly sweet, I stayed in the pack house with the smaller children and women helping make the meals, while the men were rounding the borders.

I walked into the kitchen starting to make spaghetti for tonight, I was kinda worried for Sam, but I guess according to his mother and aunt, it was alpha business and it was their problem not the womens. That's the thing about most werewolf women, they were demestic. Wanting to serve their husbands and take care of the kids, but im not most werewolf women. I have a mind of my own and I hate being put in my place by men.

I heard a bunch of yells before I seen the front door open and see Sam, his dad and a couple warrior wolves make their way into the house with the man following then.

"Oh Sam" I said running over and hugging him throwing my arms around him. He of course hugged back with ease putting his head in my hair, "We couldn't find the vampires" he said breathing in deeply "I want you to stay in this house while we search for the Vampires, just for tonight okay?" he let me go looking into my eyes.

I nodded putting my arms around his waist, as he made his way to the dining room where all the food was set , before he sat down, he raised his glass "Now before we eat this feast, I want to welcome our newcomer who shall be staying with us till we find the culprets of the attack, thank you now we shall eat." everyone yelled a couple amens and hurrays while others sat down to eat.

When Sam sat down the 'newcomer' was seated next to me eyeing me up "Hello my name is Jack and you're beautiful Luna" he said kind of gruffly but I didn't mind.

"Olivia, nice to meet you Jack" I said taking his hand which I found surprisingly cold making me flinch a bit "Are you cold?" I asked, but he shook his head.

"No, im usually this way, I feel warm as a summer nights fire, but thank you for caring Olivia" he smiled showing all of his teeth revealing two sharp canines.

I looked at his eyes then looked at my plate, "your welcome" I said before dishing up food looking over at Samuel who did the same with me, I took his hand under the table. Which I thought i heard a growl behind me but I turned to see Jack eating happily.

Jacks P.o.v

Damn that werewolf.

taking the hand of my mate, but saddly I seen the light in her eyes flicker when she looked at him, he was her mate aswell.

I growled out in hate getting a couple looks, before Olivia could look I dished up and ate my food which tasted almost vile in my mouth, god I needed meat.

I looked over at the werewolves all ripping visiously at their food while I used a fork and knife using MANNERS and eating nicely. I think Olivia noticed my nice manners cause she looked over at me smiling and said "Nice to see some manners in a house full of dogs" she then giggled, making my undead heart flip and I smiled "Yes it is, but I think in a house full of dogs there should always be a white wolf, so beautiful and intricate my dear Luna" I said eating a piece of carrot wanting to gag over the taste, but keeping a smile on my face.

She blushed a deep red and ate her food, whispering a slight thank you. I then caught the eye of the Alpha aka her mate who looked at me strangely, I only smiled back and lifted the glass of wine showing my respect though I didn't have any.

This man could burn in the deep depths of hell for taking my mate from me first. But her happiness was all in my undead heart, I wanted her to be happy even though it wouldn't be with me but a werewolf.

I'd hurt her if I killed him at this point, I could feel the love between the two. Even though I've waited for 1000 years for her....i'd wait for even longer wanting nothing more than to be next to her, to breath her beauty in and watch her.

Yes I sound like a total stalker but i didn't care. All I wanted was to be with Olivia, as a friend or lover. I will have her in the end as my own.

***

Sam's P.o.v

I found the newcomer strange, but our race takes care of any other race put in harm whether strange or not, but when he called my mate Beautiful, I almost jumped over the dining table just to interigate him.

His smell was strange and I didn't want my mates scent to be tainted by the newcomers. Once dinner was done we all made our ways into the rooms. my Beta Damion showed Jack his room, while I led Olivia to ours, which was a room I saved whenever I slept over at the pack house.

I handed one of my shirts to her, which she took and went to go get changed in my bathroom. Dang it the newcomers scent was still on her. I growled in defiance, my mate shouldn't have another males smell on her especially if it's strange.

Maybe...I could mark her? it would give the newcomer a sense of she's MINE and forever will be, it'd give him a sense to not call her beautiful.

Olivia walked out of the bathroom looking cute in my shirt, I smiled at her "Hey babe, I have a question?" I asked grabbing her waist and pulling her onto my lap.

"Yeah?" she asked looking at me closely.

I growled lightly grabbing her hair and whipping it back so her neck was barred then I whispered a sorry before I lengthened my insisers biting down on her neck. I could feel every single emotion, the one that overthrew all of them was anger.

she was angry at me for marking her, but I couldn't help being jealous of all men who looked at her, I'd apologize when she wakes up, I inserted my own little mix into her blood before letting her go and licking the mark.

But I was thinking she'd be sleeping, Nope she was looking at me her eyes a red full of anger. She got up from me smacking me right in the face "How dare you!" she yelled growling out in anger before making her way out the door.

I went to go follow her but felt the pain in her emotions and felt pain in my own heart. I sat back on the bed wanting nothing but to take it back and wait till she was ready to be marked but....my wolf didn't agree he was happy she was now officially ours.

But Olivia was still sad making us both on edge.

Chapter 13

Olivia's P.o.v

I was hurt...physically and emotionally, running down out the door I was breathing hard touching my now healing neck with tender hands. I didn't know why it hurt so much, that this happened. But saddly I did, it was because he didn't ask for my consent, it was practically mark rape.

some werewolves were killed if they did this to their mates, but I couldn't find the reason to tell anybody what he did, he was just a jelous mate and I had to understand this...but it made it harder for me to understand because of what he did.

I sat down on the porch letting the tears gush out. I pulled my legs up crying into my knees, I heard someone come outside, but I didn't care. I felt arms wrap around me and lift me up putting me in their lap and they rubbed my back calmingly.

I didn't feel the strange sparks I did that Samuel left, so I knew it was someone else and I was okay with that.

once I was done crying I lifted my head, and was met with brown eyes, definetly not Samuels but instead I was met with Jacks eyes, so mesmerizing but new. "You okay Luna?" he asked looking at my neck removing my hair from my neck, his eyes turning a dangerous red, almost blood red. That's when it hit me, he wasn't human. Not even a werewolf, he was a vampire a cold blooded vampire.

I went to scream, but I think he noticed cause he covered my mouth shaking his head back and forth covering his eyes with his blonde hair. "Please don't scream" he whispered. His eyes were pleading making me want to believe him, I felt a calming sensation come over me with him just touching me.

I breathed in and nodded, he let go of my mouth and looked at me, looking into my eyes "Please don't be scared of me Olivia....."

"Why are you here?" I got out almost stuttering, I didn't know why he was here and it was making me scared "Don't kill me" I whispered wanting to get out of his arms, but that was the thing, I couldn't I felt a pull to him....the same pull I felt toward Samuel.

I opened my eyes looking up at Jack, only to see sad eyes looking down. His arms uncoiled from around me to stay at his sides "I'd never hurt you Olivia, I think I can't hurt you without hurting myself." he said slowly touching my hair lightly putting it behind my ear.

For some strange reason I liked the touch, his hands were cold but then again....warm at the same time.

thats when I noticed in my head my wolf was now howling almost playfully Mate! another mate! I looked at Jack frowning "No, you can't be my mate" I said before getting off his lap backing away slowly "My mate is Samuel, you're a vampire, an abomination created by the devil to be damned fore ver....and I reject you because I already have a mate."

Thats when I truly looked at him, he was crushed, I could tell.

his brown eyes were now black, not a black in anger but in despair, he was silent his hands at the chairs wood looking as if he were going to rip the chair to bits, but nothing happened all that happened was a tear shed out of his eye and he stood up wrapping his arms around his waist going down the steps of the porch "Thank you, I understand now.....I won't be bothering you anymore dear Luna" he started to walk away but then fell to the ground gripping at his chest.

I watched as he threw himself to the ground, but he wasn't crying he was silently screaming toward the sky.

all that came out from his mouth was blood....much more blood then I thought could come out from a persons mouth.

I walked over to him as he fell to the ground... "Jack are you okay?" I whispered as he fell silent, just laying looking upon the sky.

"You know, vampires look for thousands of years for their mate.....that's why when we're bitten we live forever....till we find our mate....our heart begins to beat again and we continue our human cycle till our mate dies then we die along with them..... you rejected me Olivia...now I die slowly ...." he chuckled darkly clutching his heart.

"Please don't die Jack.....I just met you and I want to get to know you....." I now knew what he meant and I didn't want him to die....I knew what feeling rejected was like with Samuel...this was much worse. Dying litterally for the one you love, when they don't even love you back.

"Can you reverse this, please say you can reverse this" I whispered touching his cold chest, that's when I felt it the slow ragged breathing in his chest and a heart beat.

"kiss me" he whispered before closing his eyes.

I looked up at the bedroom window not wanting to kiss Jack at all, but if it meant saving his life I didn't care.

"Please stay alive" I bent my head down, looking at his closed eyes I bent forward more then without hesitation I kissed him, his lips were wet and sticky from his own blood, but at the same time sweet and cold against my warm and salty ones.

it was an amazing combanation, Jack then grabbing my waist pulling me closer to him, at first i didn't object because of the simple reason I felt the same pull I did with Samuel when I kissed Jack, but then it hit me right in the face.

you're not kissing Samuel.

that's when my shoulder started to burn, I let go of Jacks lips gasping as the pain expanded, I looked to my shoulder "Oh my god, it burns" I said sitting beside him, as I touched the bite which was almost already healed from the werewolf spit Samuel licked on me.

"Is it burning because I had you kiss me?" Jack asked looking at the bite and pulling my shirt's sleeve down a little bit so he could see better.

The whole bite was turning red and seething and burning, and I felt all of it hurting me all to heck when Jack touched me. "I think Sam wanted to kill me, and remind me that every time I touch another man that isn't him i'd be hurt" I said pulling up my sleeve.

I then felt a tear trickle down my cheek at the memory of why I was out here in the first place. "God I hate that he did this to me without my concent" I said growling and punching and pulling at the grass below me, "I mean would you mark your mate without her concent if you were jealous?" I asked then realized what I just said and whispered a sorry.

Jack just wiped the blood away from his mouth and looked at the starry sky "I think if I were able to have you Olivia, I'd wait till we got married and fully mated before marking you upon the wishes of tradition and you" he said before rolling on his side, propping himself up on his arm.

I smiled and laid back next to him, "You know I am sorry for not meeting you first Jack, you know that?" I said kissing his cheek, surprising him. "I think for a mate, you wouldn't be that stubborn, and overpretective" I said then I sat up, and stood up holding my hand out to him, "You know, we are mates but I don't think that prohibits us from being friends, we could have a sleepover and just hang?" I said as he grabbed my hand pulling himself up. "Cause right now I don't want to talk to or see Samuel" I continued walking toward the house holding onto Jacks hand.

He didn't complain and we walked into the house, upstairs and into his guest bedroom.

the rest of the night we just laid there watching old movies and talking about our lives.

Even though he was a vampire, and supposed to be my mate, im glad he could also be a friend when I needed one.

Chapter 14

Y ou know, I always wanted to wake up one day with sun shining in my face and just open my eyes to the one true person I loved...But today was different.

I opened my eyes to a cloudy sky, or from what I could see from the shades it was, and as soon as I looked up from the chest I lay on, I was surprised to see Jack still sound asleep. Smiling at myself I started to get up but his arm came around me hugging me to his body.

Huffing I just laid back and looked at him "Jack.....Jack wake up" I said whispering and poking his chest repeatedly.

He groaned and rolled over letting me go, before I could get up though he turned over, grabbed me and curled up "Shhhh you're warm" he whispered cuddling and putting his face in my neck. I groaned and just sat there for a while.

I turned around in his arms and giggled, if he were my mate I could tease him till he lets go..

I went to his neck and nipped and kissed till he opened his eyes groaning, and at the same time he let go, I jumped up "HA" I yelled jumping up and dancing around the room "I knew that, that would work!"

I looked over at Jack to see him smirking "You know what happens when you do that to a vampire?" he smiled at me showing off his fangs making me shiver "You shouldn't ever tease a vampire darling, it may be the last teasing you ever do" he chuckled and grabbed my arms not harshly but lightly and pulled me toward him, his face was only a couple inches away, and it seemed as if he were going to kiss me instead threw me onto the bed, and getting ontop of me starting to tickle me. I laughed so hard because it seemed like he knew where all my ticklish spots were, but before he could continue tickling me, the door flew open revealing a startled and questionable Samuel.

"What in the hell is going on here?" he hissed walking over and grabbing me out of Jacks arms, which I was in between hating and loving at the same time.

"Um I was hanging out with Jack and he ended up tickling me? isn't it obvious Alpha?" I asked seeing his annoyed glare flick over to me, then back at Jack. "What gave you the authority to mess with my Mate?" he asked holding my arm a little too tightly.

I flinched and whipped my arm out of his grip "Knock it off Sam" I said walking back over to Jack who wrapped an arm around my waist "He was just comforting me after last night, so if you wanna bite someones ear off with your rambling, why don't you go find someone else cause we were having fun and I don't need you to be biting anything else for now on" I said in one swift breath looking in his eyes the whole time, showing no wavering on my descision.

His eyes showed anything but being strong, they showed pain, anger, and jealousy but overall they showed Pain. "If that's how you feel, forget about living here go back to my house and stay there."

I stood gaping at him "Um you can't tell me what to do" I said through clenched teeth.

He chuckled "I'm your mate sweetie, I own you and the mark on your neck is proof that I do, so you get you butt out of this house and away from him before I grab you out of here and throw you out myself" he said calmly, I felt Jack stiffen next to me. I looked at him seeing his eyes switch out from brown to red in an instant.Touching his arm I noticed him calm down a fraction but not all the way, he growled before standing up "You know this may get me killed but I don't care. You never, and I mean NEVER kick your mate out of the house, especially when a guy got attacked, so if you don't mind I'm going to walk Olivia home like the mate she deserves and make sure she gets home safely so if you'll excuse me" he said before grabbing my hand, then walking out of the room me following close behind.

I looked back to see an angry looking Samuel, clenching and un-clenching his fist, GOOD he deserves Jacks words! I followed Jack almost blissfully thinking of his words.

But my Bliss was broken when an angry Samuel came running down the stairs "That was a challenge wasn't it! you were challenging me for my spot in the pack and my mate?!" he yelled pushing Jack in the process, wow he has become a total drama king since he marked me hasn't he?

Jack just chuckled and shrugged "It wasn't a challenge for you dear spot as alpha cause i don't think taking over a pack of filthy mutts would be all to well for a vampire" he smirked a snarky smirk and crossed his muscled arms.

I now noticed at this point that he wasn't the typical 'vampire' you know the pasty skinned and lanky ones everyone thinks sparkles because of the stupid Twilight movies?

no he was tanned, with bulky muscles, there wasn't much chance of telling werewolves and vampires apart.

"You're the vampire scum I smelt on the land!" Samuel yelled starting to charge for Jack, but Jack dodged at the last minute blocking me from the hit I was probably going to take.

I removed his body from mind and sidestepped him, "Samuel knock it off already!" I yelled but before I could stop him he turned into his wolf growling visiously, but that was the thing he was growling beyond me. Now that his wolf was in control, that was it for good ol' Samuel, he was gone and his wolf was in control and all he wanted to do was rip Jack to shreds.

I felt his anger, it was beyond belief and I believe if I dont get in front of him he would rip Jack into sheds.

as soon as Samuel charged for Jack, I jumped into the air into my wolf. Now that she was in control I knew she would be inbetween them both, I growled out furosiously and went in front of Jack showing I was ready to fight for him.

Samuel growled back narrowing his yellow eyes at me, but thats the thing it wasn't in anger it was in desision, he couldn't choose between killing Jack or staying back and waiting for me.He whined and got to the ground crawling over to me and licking my muzzle, a show of respect for me.

I growled and snapped my muzzle at him almost biting him in the process, I was still ticked at him from last night, and so was my wolf, she was also trying to protect her other mate.

Samuel looked into my eyes, showing he was sorry, I whined and licked his muzzle back barking at him playfully.

He stood slowly looking over at Jack and huffed before licking my muzzle repeatedly and whining, I knew he was apologizing and I loved him for that, he nodded toward the house letting me know he was going to change, I nodded my head as he made his way back to the house to change, I turned to look at Jack who looked unfazed by two giant dogs fighting over him, he probably felt so flattered.

"Well that was pretty hot" he chuckled petting my fur, making me pur under his touch. Even though he wasn't my real mate his touch felt amazing.

"Well you better go get changed before your Mate catches us touching" he chuckled backing up, and gesturing with his hands that it was okay for me to leave. I smiled a wolfy smile though I don't think he could tell, but I made my way to the house going up to our room and changing into my human form, noticing Sam was no where to be seen.

I changed into my human form feeling the crack of my bones, then I was left in my naked form. I walked to the closet opening it and grabbing my pants from the other day and Samuels shirt. Even though I couldn't stand him at that point I still needed clothing.

I finished getting dressed by putting on a pair of slippers then made my way downstairs where I seen Jack sitting on one of the couches and Samuel standing up glaring holes into Jacks head.

Walking over to Samuel I kissed his cheek and whispered a "thank you" before hugging him. He hugged back and whispered into my hair a "i'm sorry" before kissing my head. I wrapped my arms around him and kissed him lightly before letting go and walking over to Jack hugging him around his neck "Thank you for not attacking him back." and I kissed his cheek.

Both of these men were willing to stop fighting for me, and that's all that mattered to me.

That I loved both of them even though the other wasn't ever going to be like how I treat the other.

Chapter 15

J acks P.o.v

When you've spent most of your life looking for something so precious, and your faced with a werewolf that could kill you, you just stand you ground.

I wanted Olivia as a friend at this point and Samuel was going to put her out of safety just to stay away from me? What kind of mate would do that! It ticked me off that he marked her in general and even worse without her consent? even worse UGH!

In the morning after yesterday I walked into the kitchen wanting to get some food when I walked in to see little Olivia slaving over the stove looking absolutely exhausted and as if she'd been working since dawn since she had purple bags under her eyes "You know, a beautiful women is a symbol for beauty....I'm thinking that if your going to slave over a stove you should at least be baking instead of messing with all that grease" I said with ease leaning against the door frame, loving my view.

Yes, in the morning I can be a big perve. But who cares? im a guy.... a vampire but still a guy in all sense of mind.

I heard Olivia giggle, sounding like an angel from up in the heavens, "Oh yeah okay, even then i'd still be sweating like a pig and you'd say the same exact thing" she said turning around and putting pieces of greased overcooked pig strips on the plate, I gulped in distaste and turned my head away.Olivia of course noticed because she smirked "You don't like Bacon? what creature doesn't like Bacon?" she asked looking at me confuzed, her eyebrows going together quizically.

I shrugged "if it were raw, sure I'd love it. To suck whatever blood remained." I said sliding into a bar stool, watching as she made a discusted face then went back to cooking.

I chuckled and watched as a very tired looking Alpha walked into the kitchen grumbling and sliding in the bar stool next to me putting his head upon the table. Olivia walked over putting a mug of coffee in front of him and walking over kissing his cheek, then she walked over to me and handing me a mug of coffee, but then I smelt the pleasant smell of blood tang in the coffee.

"Olivia, dear. You did not put your blood in my coffee? did you" I asked putting the tainted coffee on the table. Samuels tired face snapped up, looking at Olivia saddly and back at me glaring through his eyelashes.

Olivia giggled and shook her head "I rung out the beef we have in the fridge so you can get some blood in you, even if it's raw blood with coffee." she said smirking and walking over to Samuel who looked almost discusted before he said "At least it's not my mates blood" he smiled kissing her cheek.

I looked away sipping my coffee, as it actually tasted pretty good. I got up and stretched "Im going to go get dressed then go into town to find a house" I said going toward the stairs, but was stopped by a familiar voice "Why? I thought you were staying here?" Olivia asked rushed.

I turned around and saw Samuel glaring and rolled my eyes "Sorry darlin, your boyfriend wouldn't like the competition" I said before going upstairs to my 'room' and getting dressed in black jeans and a black button up T-shirt, I walked to the mirror seeing my thin but toned self and fluffed up my blonde hair, you know for being 1017 I looked pretty good.

I chuckled grabbing my leather jacket before going downstairs seeing the love birds on the couch watching a show I had no interest in. I walked to the front door seeing a couple werewolf males outside training, I walked out going toward the dirt trail that led to town. When I got further down the train I crouched down and started to run.

I sprinted feeling the wind whip around me, trees hit my face but the tiny cuts healed as soon as they were made.

I loved to run, it was the only passtime where I couldn't feel the pain of 1017 years way in on me, I felt absolutely free. When I was turned, I had just turned 17 me and my friends had a huge party, you know the deal, beer, music,hot chicks. But instead of regular girls, we decided to have some fun and invite these random chicks from a bar that we had just met.

We brought them back to the apartment, thinking we'd just have some fun with them before they gone back home.

that wasn't the case sadly in the end I brought back one of the girls named Elizebeth and was kissing her, but the thing was she went for my neck and bit, before I knew it I was dead on the floor, blood surrounding me.

I was dead and a vampire.

that was the last time I heard my heart beat, or ate something without blood, without taste in fact.

Interrupting my thoughts I focused in front of me as I entered town. Walking into town I wondered if I would find an apartment or house in a town of 300 people.

Small towns= no houses available.

But I kept looking to no avail.

****

Olivia's P.O.V

As soon as Jack left, Samuel's tension came off as well, he ate the food I made and we cuddled up on the couch watching simple shows, such as Chopped.

"do you actually think he's your mate Olivia?" Sam asked wrapping his arms around. I looked at my hands worried about what he'd think about my responce If I responded.

I bit my lip looking up at him "Well... I feel the same way I do about him, that I do with you." I said shakilly before hiding my face away from him, I didn't want to face those cold blue eyes.

Though I didn't feel him pull my hands away from my face, which I hoped he would. Instead I felt him get up from the couch taking my legs off his lap, I peeked through my hands to see him making his way up the stairs.

"Sam, what are you doing?" I asked standing up, starting to walk toward him. He swung around almost looking as if he were going to be in tears.

"You know what Olivia." he paused wiping at his eyes "I thought...I thought for one second, just one that I could live happilly with you in the future with our how ever many kids that we want to have....but No he has to come in the picture saying a bunch of crap that's just pulling you in, and you're falling for it, he's doing shit to make you come to him and it's stupid." he turned around as soon as a tear fell down.

Looking at his back I wanted to run after him, but what he said hurt "So you think our relationship is stupid? Cause he's doing exactly what you did to louer me in" I said looking down at the floor. Before I could back away, I felt two hands on both sides of my face, I looked up stricken by the eyes that stared at me so intensily.

"Dont.Ever.Say.That.Again" He whispered out rubbing my temples with his thumbs making me calm with just the feel of him. "I never ever, said our relationship is stupid. I'd never say that for it'd kill me inside more than it would before." he said his eyes wavering, but still looking into mine "I love you Olivia, I'm a jealous jerk and I wish I weren't but it worsen's with the change." He smirked looking down at me "And now that we're officially together, you're making me jealous every single day, and it's making the jealousy worse" he smiled and kissed my cheek "I love you and i'm sorry about last night, that was the jealous jerk in me, peeking out" he said smiling then kissing me lightly.

Even though it was light and not that long, all of his lovely words were spoken by them, and I felt all that love, and it was strong.

I smiled and wrapped my arms around his neck, pulling him closer then I kissed him but instead of lightly, it was passionate showing my forgiveness.

pulling away he nodded putting his head against mine "Your forgive me then?" He asked. I smiled and nodded before taking his hand and going upstairs.

I wanted to show him that I forgave him, and now that I had the mating mark on my neck I needed to give mine then we could 'finish' the process.

****

Yes it is what you're thinking, lol use your imagination my readers.

I love you guys so much, thank you for reading, this chapter is finally out.

Chapter 16

J ack's P.o.v

I walked home, feeling sad because I was simply out of luck. No apartments or houses were for sale, and saying that the whole town were werewolves, I couldn't use compulsion to get a room or an apartment.

I walked back to the pack house wanting to go back to my residence and take a shower, without any interuption.I walked up the porch stairs almost slugishly, some werewolf women looking at me and winking. But I just smirked at them then looked forward in disgust.

Walking up the stairs I was almost to my room when all the sudden I smacked into someone, sending shocks into my body. I looked up at her and smiled, but my smiled faultered when I seen she was in a small pink bathroad, her hair wet going down her back.

But that wasn't all I noticed, she smelt different, not just from her mark from her douchebag of a mate, but in fact that they had finished the process while I was gone.

I growled storming toward my room, Olivia calling my name, but I wasn't listening. My heart was in my ears and I couldn't barely hear her. How dare she?! I'm also her mate for god sakes, and she does this?? Walking swiftly to my room I finally stopped at the door and looked at her.

she almost ran into my body as she was running to catch up to me "Please Jack understand, I never knew you before Sam. I love him because I've known him longer, I love you as a friend and a mate, but Samuel was going to reject me tonight." she was practically in tears as she begged for my forgiveness. But i'd never forgive her, I think she knew that.

I growled and shook my head "i'll forgive you, but i'm getting the heck out of this house, where I don't have to see you and your "mate" makeout all the time" I walked into my room not caring of her answer.

But the thing was, when I closed the door upon that beautiful face.

I died inside my heart breaking twice as much as it should of. I clenched my chest, tearing running down my pale face. I've never cried so hard in my 1000 years.

I practically died as the sun went down, the orange streaks on the floor turning to black as I whimpered and sobbed out my feelings. Sometimes Olivia would come to the door to see if I was okay.

I'd never answer, for I didn't want her to know that I was suffering, from her impractical descision.

****

Olivia's P.o.v

I know that he said that he forgave me but the thing was, I felt his heart be ripped out as soon as he shut the door. He never came out after that, not when I asked him to come to dinner, not when I asked to see if he was okay, he never answered but I heard the choked sobs.

I think he practically died in that room, but not litterally, I never rejected him. Just told him i'd love him as a friend and a mate.

After he shut the door on me, I walked downstairs and sat on the stairs wanting to cry, but the tears wouldn't come.

Samuel was now running the borders, so I couldn't look for comfort in him. But what comfort would I get if he was my mate.

I needed Jeremy and he was gone.

I took out my phone pressing Jeremy's phone number putting it to my ear, thinking i'd get a voice mail.

but instead I got his caring voice "Olivia, I'm so sorry I haven't been answering, sweetie i'm here for you" he said finally.

and i broke down, tears splashed down my cheeks in a waterfall "Jer...I need...a talk...to you......" I whimpered out wiping my tears away "you..'ve been gone...and a bunch of crap has happend...im hurting Jeremy" I finally got out before I sniffled and whined.

"i'm here for ya baby girl just calm down, where are you?" he asked sounding out of breath.

"i'm at Samuels pack house, we moved he as soon as you left." I said pulling my knees to my chest. I heard the phone disconect, I looked down and my eyes widened the phone hung up.

But as soon as it did the door wipped open my darling brother came in looking sweaty as ever.

At the point I didn't care whether or not Jeremy was sweaty, and I had just taken a shower ran up to him hugging him tightly "I missed you so much Jer" I whined into his shoulder gripping his shirt in my hands.

"I missed you too"

Chapter 17

J eremy's P.o.v

You know. I'd never thought I'd stoop this low.....to go and find my little sister and bring her to my alpha, a rogue from the western borders.

Yes..I was a rogue, when Stephanie died I practically died inside, running through the woods till I fell to the ground going through a transition, my wolf looked muddy now with red eyes, Not like my brown ones.

Being a rogue was better, going against the rules, killing goody two shoes wolves for our own pleasure. My alpha wanted Olivia, and I was willing to give her up. Don't think me a terrible person cause im not. I only saw red and tasted blood as I bit my tongue in distaste of my little baby sister.

"You know, I'm only here for the week, so you needa explain what's been going on so I can get the hell outta here" I said growling as I grabbed Olivia off me. I could see the saddness in her eyes but I didn't look for long when a man with sandy blonde hair came walking down the stairs looking mopy and just plain old sad.

Then he saw me and growled out, not a normal wolf growl but a different animal entirely. I backed away from Olivia as I saw the guy making his way toward us, not looking sappy anymore, no he looked alert and ready to attack me.

"So now you freaking go after a rogue! when will it end??? you go for a merman next!" He yelled at Olivia, my eyes widened when he said rogue. He could sense me? how could he?

Olivia's eyes went to me then back to the guy then toward the ground "Is this true Jeremy?" she asked, but saddly I couldn't answer because Samuel walked in looking sweaty and gross. I didn't want to be around when he came in, that would be the point of no return for them knowing I was a rogue.

This one guy knew I was one, but Samuel knowing as well would send Olivia over the edge. Olivia looked at me with hurt, but I didn't care I growled out defensively at the blondey and tranformed howling to the morning air.

Olivias face went from hurt to horror in one quick look, and she was behind Samuel who looked as if he were going to rip my head off at any second.

Thats when I saw it, the blonde came running at me from the side grabbing my side smashing me into a tree, I heard a crack but ignored the pain, whoever this guy was he hasn't fought a rogue like me before, I let out a menacing growl before getting up and wrapping my jaw around his wrist snapping it. But as soon as his blood spilt on my tongue I wanted to puke, it tasted like tar.

He smiled at me taking his wrist and snapping it back into place before taking an attack stance, I now realized what he was Vampire

I growled at him before looking at Olivia then the woods, I took off into the woods knowing, now that there was a vampire involved the plan wasn't going to work as well. I ran till I hit the western boarder.

Olivia's P.o.v

I watched as my big brother turned into a muddy haired, red eyed wolf. I started breathing as he was going to attack but Jack got in front of me protectively showing his fangs. I slowly went to the ground feeling like I was going to be sick or worse, faint.

The wolf that used to be my brother took one glance at me before howling and running into the woods leaving a grimy bloody steanch in the air. As soon as he was gone, I got up running behind a tree puking up everything that was in my stomach.

I felt two hands go on my back one both of them I felt electric shocks knowing that it was otherwise Jack or Sam. I finish puking standing up both hands still on my back, I turn around seeing both Samuel and Jack standing looking at me worried.

"Olivia. Are you okay darling?" Sam asked putting his hands on my shoulders, as Jack kept his hand on my waste, keeping me steady.

I shook my head not wanting to speak cause my mouth tasted gross. I took Sam's hands off my shoulders before going inside of the house, where it was a little trashed. Walking up the stairs I felt almost numb. Going to my room I laid down on my bed letting the tears finally come, three things rushed through my head.

1: my heart was completely and utterly broken

2: I have two mates

3: My big brother was a rogue and wanted me for something.

I wasn't normal to say the least, and I couldn't stand the idea.

As the day went on I got multiple knocks on the door, even from my parents who knew nothing of Jeremy. I cried myself asleep wanting nothing but this to be a terrible nightmare I could wake up from and have my brother hugging me and telling me the good and bad things of boys, and that if any boy ever hurts me, he'd kill them.

I missed my big brother and he was never coming back not as my big brother anyways.

I wallowed in my saddness for what seemed like hours.

Chapter 18

Jacks P.o.v

As I watched my mate walk up to her room, knowing that she had been hurt from the pain she had to go through today, I seemed to feel her pain. Samuel came in after telling his mom and dad about the attack, he looked at me and gave me a smug grin "I wanted to tell you, thank you for protecting Olivia" he said holding his hand out for me to shake.

I shook it then letting go crossing my arms over my chest "I'd do anything for her Samuel, even if we're both her mates and she has chosen you, saddly to say....I'd still protect her with my life" I said giving him a grim smile before making my way upstairs to my room.

I sat on my bed grabbing my small bag from under the bed. I took out a bottle of whiskey downing a couple gulps before swallowing and looking at the floor. The sad thing about alcohol, was that for vampires it did nothing, simply gave us a small buz then it was gone in seconds.

After I turned I couldn't simply face the fact that I was a blood sucking monster, Every night i'd down about 3 bottles of whiskey before going out to suck innocent peoples blood. For the couple years of my life I was what they called a shredder I'd kill and drink with no recolect or care for the persons life. I was in simpler words, a monster. I found out that vampires can have mates when I was 10 years into my new life, I stopped drinking, taking a bag and traveling about the world traveling the whole globe for millenia till I found her, I didn't care if she was a werewolf, all I cared about was that she was mine, Apart of my undead heart.

But....that bastard had to keep his claws tucked into her and she followed, getting marked and mated before even giving me a full chance. My love was hurting now, and she wanted nothing to do with me.

I took another sip a tear slipping down my face. Taking the empty bottle I smashed it on the wall, making it shatter into tiny pieces.

I growled and laid back on the bed wondering about today, who the boy was and how he knew Olivia. I shouldn't have said what I said though.. I regreted that the most. Hearing the door click open I jumped up, stood in front of me was the small form of Olivia looking fragile and sad. She looked at the broken glass then me giving me a sad smile, she walked over to me sitting in my lap and wrapping her arms around my neck. "Jack...I wanted to say thank you for protecting me today" she whispered her voice cracking.

Tucking her face into my neck I felt her tears falling, and her soft cries vibrating my chest. Switching positions I laid back with her next to me her head on my chest "Shhhh, Olive, shhhh" I whispered kissing her head.

She silenced for a while, followed by soft snoring signaling she was asleep. Looking over at her my thoughts were confirmed seeing a sleeping angel in my bed. I smiled kissing her head, then looking down at her lips I smiled, I kissed her lightly before starting to get up with her in my arms.

I walked out of my bedroom going toward hers.

Walking into her room I lay her in her bed ready to leave but her arms stayed around me tight. I frowned and laid down next to her, getting as comfortable I was aloud to. This was untouchable territory but, I didn't care I wanted to comfort her for the night, even if she wasn't awake.

I fell asleep after a while, with my darling heart in my arms, wishing I had a camera to take a picture so I didn't have to say goodbye to this moment.

Chapter 19

Olivia's P.o.v

The first thing I smelt in the morning was a musky manly smell surrounding me, I opened my eyes to find myself looking at black material.

Shifting up so I could see better I seen the shirt was on a guy, Jack to be specific. I felt a small tingly sensation when I touched his chest dragging my finger down his chest to his abs. I smiled content and laid back down in his arms feeling at bliss, just being in his arms kept me calm.

I took a deep breath before closing my eyes, but before I could go back to sleep I felt Jack move beneath me, my wolf whined making me whine a bit aswell clinging onto his warm and muscled arm.

I felt his chest vibrate as he settled back into the bed, "I have to get up Olive" he whispered kissing my head.

"I know, but I don't want you too" I whispered wraping my legs around his. His chest vibrated underneath me once more before he started getting up again "Your boyfriend would be pretty mad, if I kept you in this bed" I opened my eyes and looked at him glaring then let go of him entirely.

"Fine i'm taking over your bed as soon as you leave then" I smiled up at him as he got up from the bed, smirking down at me "God you're making this harder, and harder for me to leave aint ya?" he said running his fingers through his dirty blonde hair.

"Yep cause your leaving me here, cold and alone in this huge bed" I fake pouted then rolled over burrying my face in his pillows "But I guess your pack work is far more important than your parcial mate" I said as it was muffled by the pillows.

I felt the bed dip and a body laying on top of mine, I giggled as I felt Jack burry his face in my neck, his breath tickling it, "stop making this harder than it should be, I'm in pain every time I see you with that prick, so don't even play the parcial mate card. I may have saved you yesterday, but im not your protector, the one you chose to be your mate is. So don't make this harder for me then it is" he growled out then got off me, I heard his feet patter across the room till I heard the door open and slam shut.

Gosh...We made him mad, my wolf whimpered, but I had to agree with her, we made Jack mad and we couldn't take anything back.

I rolled back onto my back feeling tears prick at my eyes.

***

God that damn she-wolf! sometimes I hated that we have this dang mate connection, if we didn't I think i'd leave here completely forgetting this stupid pack. I growled as I walked down the stairs seeing Samuel at the end of them in the living room, sitting there as if he were waiting for the black screen of the Tv to change.

I passed him by as I smirked then I walked straight out the door to the yard where some wolves were practicing their fighting tecnique.

On the sidelines a couple she-wolf pack slutts sat watching the men work out, I smiled and walked over kneeling next to them, "Hello ladies, and how are you this fine morning?" they turned their head cocking their heads to the side as if wondering why I was there.

A blonde with brown eyes and a nose piecing got up and started toward me "Very good and how is yours sexy" she said trying to use a seductive tone in her voice, I put my hands on her hips as she put her hands on my chest looking at my lips. I bent down a little and without a care of no body thought, I kissed her feeling a slight pain in my chest but it wasn't as bad as the pain from having my mate torn away from me.

As I kissed her my fangs started growing almost ripping at her bottom lip, but I pulled away before they could and smirked at her, "so have you ever wanted to be bitten by a vampire darling?" I asked seeing as she was probably a total die hard twilight fan. It was false to think that if a vampire bit a werewolf that they'll die, their blood just taste a little bit more bitter than another vampires or a humans.I seen the sparkle in her eyes, then I could hear her heart start beating faster. She nodded and grabbed my hand pulling me toward the house once more, pulling me up the stairs to im guessing her room, covered in pink and glitter. Walking to her bed she sat down flipping her blonde curls to the side and putting her head back offering her neck to me, where I saw a pulsing vein.

I growled before striding over, not caring that the door to the bedroom wasn't closed. I put one of my hands in her hair ready to pull if she struggled. As I did this, I plunged my fangs into her pale flesh feeling her skin rip underneath them, her blood splashed my tongue making me moan in satisfaction. As she started to make a little bit more noise I covered her mouth with my free hand yanking her hair.

She moaned as I sucked more, sending my special mix of chemicals into her so she was left in a blood lust and forgot that I ever bit her, before releasing her completely, letting her fall into the bed limp her eyes swirling.

"Thanks darling, go to sleep. Once you wake up you'll find your neck hurts but bandage it up and tell no one." she nodded and swallowed, not out of fear but from that she couldn't speak. I bent down kissing her forehead and turning around to go the way I came but what or I guess who stood in front of me stopped me in my tracks.

Olivia stood in almost shock, "You....you just bit her." she whispered grabbing the door jamb for support. I didn't know if it were a statement or a question, all I knew is she saw it.

You'd think i'd be absolutely torn, or feel some sort of guilt. No. I felt the exact opposite, I felt accomplished and I felt great.

"Yes I bit her, and sucked her blood. I am a vampire Olivia, you should understand that werewolves are not the only supernatural being in this world of yours and that I have to suck the blood of others to stay alive, so forget even telling your precious mate that I did this, cause I'll be out the door in the morning if you do." I growled out as I grabbed her shoulders lifting her and putting her aside as I walked out the way I came, wiping my mouth.

I felt so accomplished, cause now she hated me. My heart suffered enough to know she'd come crawling back into my arms as soon as Samuel did anything to her, but this time I hope she never crawled into my arms now that she seen how much of her mate was a monster.

I was a monster.

And she deserved better.

Chapter 20

S amuels Point of view:

You know that feeling where every single wrong thing you hope doesn't happen, happens. It feels as if your world is crashing around yo u.God I felt as if I lost Olivia forever, and I couldn't handle it. I heard a door slam upstairs but I didn't look, I just stared at the black screen.

I heard upstairs a door slam, I didn't move not even move but I knew that Jack was coming down the stairs. I watched as he exited out the door.

God I hated the thought of him being so close to Olivia, when she was supposed to be my mate. Walking to the kitchen I grabbed a beer then walked out of the house not caring that half of my pack mates were watching as their "Glorious" alpha crumbling in front of them.

Drinking the beer down in one gulp I got down on all fours not caring that if I had clothes on or not I jumped into my wolf form lunging into running. God I was so mad I thought my head would pop off my furry shoulders. Then I smelt it, that sickly sweet smell that I only smelt when around Jack.

Vampire

It was very close, but smelling almost ill. I slowed my pace, smelling it get stronger, but as I got closer my hair raised on my back. I came through the bushes to see a scene that made bile rise up to the back of my throat, and made me want to rip apart everything in site.

3 vampires stood feasting upon a she-wolf, to be specific, my sister. Her eyes were blank and her brown fur stained with blood as the vampires feasted upon her. Growling I lunged forward taking the first vampire from behind the neck cutting off his wind pipe and cracking his neck, next I lunged for another behind me ripping his stomach out.

I felt my anger radiating off me and it burned hot.

As I ripped into the vampires hating them with every inch of my being, I couldn't stop as I slaughtered all of the vampires who killed my little sister. As soon as I was done I laid down next to my sister feeling as if my heart had broken.

I whined and whimpered as I stood up licking my sister cheek, then I ran into the woods heading toward home, I wanted to kill the vampire scum in my house and I wanted him dead now; even if he loved my mate and she loved him, I wanted him dead.

As I entered the house changed in my human form in just shorts I walked upstairs past my mother and father before grabbing the neck of my enemy and threw him off the stairs "How dare you!" I growled out as Olivia came out of her room in two towels wrapped around her body and hair.

"What the hell Sam!" she yelled running down toward the cowered.

I growled and shook as I walked down "Vampires invaded the area and killed my baby sister because of this fucking scumback living in my house, now I want him out or im going to kill him!" I yelled grabbing him by the back of his neck and carrying him with ease outside, only to hear the anguish of my mothers screams before I shut the door behind us as I threw the vampire scum to the ground kicking him in his gut. "Get the hell out of my territory"

Jack looked at me with almost fear in his eyes, looking over at my mate which made my blood boil even more; he stood his arms at his sides "I'm sorry for your loss, even if I didn't help with the fault, I am sorry and will leave." He didn't say anything but look at Olivia once before making his exit toward the woods.

My blood boiled and I didn't want to talk to anyone, I walked passed a shocked Olivia before walking into the house seeing my parents huddled up on the couch. Walking over to them I bent over hugging my mom "I'm sorry I couldn't have saved her" I whispered before standing and walking upstairs.

As I got passed my door and shut it, I broke down into a sea of oblivion

Losing someone is like grabbing a pliars and ripping your heart out. I Samuel will set fire to the vampire cults as soon as I become full alpha, with out without Olivia in line with me.